for Riley

A Doubleday Book for Young Readers

Published by
Bantam Doubleday Dell Publishing Group, Inc.
1540 Broadway
New York, New York 10036

Doubleday and the portrayal of an anchor with a dolphin are trademarks of
Bantam Doubleday Dell Publishing Group, Inc.

Library of Congress Cataloging–in–Publication Data

Haynes, Max.
    In the driver's seat / Max Haynes.
        p.   cm.
    Summary: A driving lesson becomes a wild ride through
countryside and city streets, with an unexpected conclusion.
        ISBN 0-385-32502-9
        [1. Automobiles—Fiction.]   I. Title.
PZ7.H3149149In   96–37215
[E]—DC21   CIP
                                                          AC

Manufactured in the United States of America
October 1997
10 9 8 7 6 5 4 3 2 1

IN THE DRIVER'S SEAT

BY MAX HAYNES

A Doubleday Book for Young Readers

Okay, start the engine and rev it up.
Brrrroom, Brrrroom!
Now wave good-bye, and off we go*ooooooooo.*

Let's go fast. I mean *really* fast!
Zzzzooooom!
Quick, lean to your left. Turn, turn, turn!

Yikes! Look out for that cow!

Mooooo!

Turn right, right, right! *Rrrrrrrrrrrrt.*

Bluck, bluck, block!
Uh-oh, now we're driving through a barn.
Hee-haw, Hee-haw!

B-b-b-boy, this mountain trail
sure is *b-b-b*-bumpy.
I can't read that sign up ahead.

Oh no! It said ROAD CLOSED.
Now we're heading straight for the lake.
Lean back, hold your nose, and get ready!

SPLASH!
Let's hurry before we fill up with water.
Blub, blub, blub.

Quack, quack.

Hey, you silly ducks, get off the car!

Scare them away by going into that tunnel.

Now we're heading into the big city.
Can you hear the traffic noise?
Beep, beeeep! **Honk, honk.**

Stop! Always do what the policewoman says.
Even if she points you straight into
a *roaring* car race!

Vaaa-rooom!
Turn to the right. Turn to the left.
Pass those cars. Faster, faster!

You won the race! There's your trophy.
Hip, hip, hooray!
Not bad for your first driving lesson!